Mine Your Business

The green leaves of palm trees swayed in the breeze as Ash and his friends got ready for lunch. May and her little brother, Max, sat at the white picnic table. Brock stood at the head table over a pile of food. He was making sandwiches.

A group of hungry Pokémon lined up in front of the table, waiting to eat.

"Pikachu!" cried Ash's yellow Electric-type Pokémon.

"Torchic!" chirped May's little orange Pokémon.

"Forretress," said Brock's Pokémon, from inside its hard shell.

Ash's Flying-type Pokémon flapped its wings. *"Taillow!"*

"Corphish! Phish! Phish!" said Ash's Water-type Pokémon. It clicked its claws excitedly.

"Okay, everyone, calm down," Brock said. "Lunch will be ready soon. How about helping me with the salad, Corphish?"

"Corphish!" the red Pokémon said happily.

"Start by cutting the veggies," Brock said.

Corphish waved its sharp, crablike claws. In a flash, it chopped up a pile of cucumbers, tomatoes, and onions.

"Awesome!" said Max.

Then Corphish crawled over to the pile of sandwiches.

"No, Corphish!" May warned. "Not the sandwiches!"

But Corphish didn't listen. It wanted to show off.

Swish! Swish! Swish! In just seconds, Corphish chopped up the sandwiches until there was nothing left but a pile of tiny crumbs.

There was no way to save the sandwiches. Brock

2

POKÉMON

Haunted!

By Tracey West

SCHOLASTIC INC.
New York   Toronto   London   Auckland   Sydney
Mexico City   New Delhi   Hong Kong   Buenos Aires

ISBN 0-439-80001-3

Published by Scholastic Inc.
SCHOLASTIC and associated logos are trademarks and/or registered trademarks of Scholastic Inc.

12 11 10 9 8 7 6 5 4 3 2   6 7 8 9 10/0

Designed by Bethany Dixon
Printed in the U.S.A.
First printing, January 2006

put a pile of crumbs on each plate and gave everyone a spoon.

"Corphish, this is all your fault," Ash said glumly. "I hope you at least feel bad about it."

But Corphish just grinned. *"Corphish!"*

Max frowned. "I'd say from that happy face that Corphish doesn't feel bad at all."

Ash shook his head. Corphish was a good Pokémon, but it joked around too much. And it didn't listen to Ash the way it should.

"I've got to do something about Corphish's attitude," Ash grumbled. "And fast!"

Not far away, Jessie, James, and Meowth were walking in a hilly area. The three members of Team Rocket were never far from Ash and his friends. That's probably because they were still trying to steal Ash's Pokémon, Pikachu — or any other Pokémon they could get their hands on.

Team Rocket stopped at the base of a hill, near the open mouth of a cave.

"James, where are we?" Jessie wailed. "Check the map."

James studied the paper map in his hands. "Well, according to this, we're looking at an old gold mine."

Meowth's eyes lit up. "At some point, this place must have been a mountain of treasure!"

"Treasure mountain?" Jessie said. "Now you're speaking my language. Imagining building my dream house using nothing but gold bricks!"

"But, Jessie, this mine closed a long time ago," James pointed out. "There isn't any gold left."

"There's got to be something left," Jessie said, her blue eyes gleaming. "I smell the sweet smell of success!"

"I'm picking up that happy smell, too," Meowth said. "If we find gold, and give it to the Boss . . ."

". . . We'll get a big promotion!" Jessie finished.

James was convinced. They headed into the cave. Jessie's strange blue Pokémon, Wobbuffet, popped out of its Poké Ball and followed them.

The tunnel leading to the mine was dark and narrow.

They soon came to a dark red mining cart sitting on a track that led deeper into the cave. Team Rocket jumped into the cart and pulled a lever. The cart slowly rolled down the track.

It traveled deeper and deeper into the tunnel. The tunnel got darker and darker. A cold chill crept around them.

James shivered. "Maybe we should leave this creepy cave."

"I bet this joint is haunted!" Meowth said, looking fearfully at the dark shadows on the cave walls.

"Cool it, Meowth," Jessie said. "You know how that stuff scares James — what's that?"

Two glowing white lights floated in the darkness ahead of them.

"Now I'm scared," James whispered.

A low, gravelly voice filled the cave.

"*Sableye,*" the voice moaned.

The glowing lights floated toward them. As they got closer, they looked like two eyes. Then a mouth of white teeth glowed in the darkness under the eyes.

"Sableye!" the voice growled.

"A ghost!" Jessie yelled.

"Mommy, help me!" James wailed.

James pulled the lever on the mining cart. The cart sped back in reverse. But the jolt sent Meowth flying out of the cart.

"Don't leave me!" Meowth cried. But Jessie, James, and Wobbuffet disappeared into the darkness.

Panicked, Meowth looked up at the ghost. It jumped right in front of Meowth. Meowth could see a shadowy dark figure with two legs, two glowing eyes, and shining white teeth.

"Heeeeelp!" Meowth screamed.

Then it tripped and passed out.

The Friendly Ghost Pokémon

After lunch, Ash led his friends to the abandoned gold mine. He had found it on a map, just as James had. But Ash had a different idea than looking for old treasure.

"This will be the perfect place to do our training," Ash said.

"What do you mean by that, Ash?" Brock asked.

Ash grinned. "You'll see. Let's go inside."

They walked inside the cave. Pikachu rode on Ash's shoulder. Ash kept the rest of his Pokémon inside their Poké Balls. He didn't need them — yet.

"It sure is spooky in here," May said, as they made their way down the dark tunnel.

"Exactly," Ash said. "We'll get a big scare into Corphish. After a good scare, maybe Corphish will settle down a whole bunch. You'll see."

Max shook his head. "I'll be amazed if that works."

"Here's how it'll work," Ash said confidently. He explained his plan. When he finished, May looked impressed.

"I think your plan might actually work," she said.

"So, are you in, Max?" Ash asked.

Max sighed. "I guess!"

Ash smiled. "Thanks, guys! I knew I could count on you!"

While Ash worked out his plan, Meowth woke up from its faint. It found itself in a white room. Lights flickered on the ceiling. And in front of Meowth was — the ghost!

"Aaaah!" Meowth shrieked. But then it stopped. The figure in the tunnel wasn't a ghost at all — it was a Pokémon!

"Hey, you're a Sableye, ain't ya!" Meowth realized.

"*Sableye!*" the Pokémon replied.

"I'm glad I know my Pokémon," Meowth said. It knew that Sableye was a combination Dark-and-Ghost-type Pokémon. In the light, Meowth could make out its whole body: a big head; large, silver eyes shaped like gems; pointy ears; and a red jewel in its belly. Its smooth skin was dark purple.

Then Sableye began to talk. Meowth could understand the language of other Pokémon.

"So you're saying that ya just like scaring humans and ya didn't mean to hurt us," Meowth translated.

"*Sableye, Sableye!*"

Then Sableye took a bite of something in its hand.

"I didn't eat all day," Meowth said.

Sableye nodded and handed Meowth a piece of what it was eating. Meowth bit down and . . . "Ouch!" Meowth yelled. "That's a rock!"

Sableye grinned. "*Sableye.*"

"It wasn't that funny," Meowth complained.

Sableye started talking again. Meowth translated. Sableye said it was lonely in the cave and wanted

Meowth to stick around. The white room they were in was the old control room from back in the days when the mine was working. Windows gave a view of the tunnels below.

Suddenly, Meowth saw something moving in the tunnels.

"Uh-oh!" Meowth cried. It was Max and May, riding in a mining cart. "Dat's a couple of them twerps out there!"

"Sableye, Sableye, Sableye!" Sableye said.

"You want me to help you play a practical joke on them?" Meowth translated.

Meowth started to get an idea. Meowth could pretend to be friends with Sableye. Then Sableye could help Meowth find the gold.

"Then I can give the gold to the Boss, and he'll give me a promotion before Jessie and James!" Meowth said to itself. It turned to Sableye.

"Ya got yourself a deal!" Meowth said. "Let's scare 'em!"

Too Many Tricks

3

"I hope Max and May are ready to go," Ash said, as he walked down the track leading into the gold mine. Pikachu perched on his shoulder.

Ash stopped. He took a Poké Ball from his belt and threw it in the air.

"Corphish, I choose you!"

Corphish popped out of the Poké Ball. It began to wave its claws, ready for battle.

"We're not battling this time," Ash told it. "Today, we'll be testing your courage. It's time to check out what you're made of by exploring this creepy cave."

"*Corphish, phish phish!*" the little Pokémon chuckled.

"Are you making fun of me?" Ash asked.

Corphish nodded.

"You'd better watch that attitude," Ash warned. "It's been said there are ghosts down here, you know."

Nearby, Max and May hid behind a mining trolley. On cue, they began to wail like a ghost.

"Oooooooooooh!"

"Hey, that sounds like a ghost now," Ash said loudly.

Max climbed onto May's shoulders. Then he draped a long white sheet over them. They looked like a tall ghost. Then they walked out of the darkness toward Corphish.

"I'm a ghost," Max said. "Boooooooo!"

Corphish began to sweat and wave its claws wildly. Ash could see it was scared.

"It's working!" Ash said under his breath. "Corphish is so scared!"

Corphish looked terrified. Then, without warning, it jumped up and slammed into Max and May!

"Hey!" they screamed.

They tumbled backward, falling into the mining cart,

which rolled down the track. The sheet fell off of them. Corphish saw that it had been tricked. It turned and gave Ash an angry look.

"*Corphish!*" it said. Then it ran off down one of the tunnels.

"Corphish, come back!" Ash yelled. "That's not the way out of here!"

Ash ran down the tunnel after Corphish. Max and May sat up in the mining cart.

"I had no idea Corphish would attack us," May said.

"Let's get out of here," Max said.

But before they could climb out of the cart, Sableye jumped onto the cart's edge. Its eyes glowed with eerie white light.

"*Sableye!*" it growled.

"Aaaaaaaah!" Max and May screamed. "It's a ghost!"

"*Sableye,*" the Pokémon repeated.

"Hey, wait a minute," Max said. "That's not a ghost, May. It's just a Sableye, a Pokémon."

"Sableye?" May had never heard that name before. She quickly took out her Pokédex, a small computer that held information about all kinds of Pokémon. A picture of Sableye appeared on the screen.

"Sableye, the Darkness Pokémon," said the Pokédex. "Sableye normally live deep within caves and eat rocks. They use their sharp claws to dig through the earth."

Sableye laughed. Max and May had actually thought it was a ghost! It loved fooling humans.

Max got angry. "We were almost scared to death, and Sableye thinks it's funny!"

"You're right," May agreed. "Here we are thinking we see a ghost, and Sableye's just laughing!"

May took out a Poké Ball. "I'll show you. Torchic, come out!"

May's little Fire-type Pokémon popped out of its ball. It looked like a cute orange bird. But it packed lots of fire power.

"Torchic, teach Sableye a lesson with Ember, now!" May cried.

Torchic opened its beak. Sableye jumped up and hung upside-down from the ceiling.

Hot embers flew from Torchic's beak. They showered the ceiling like fiery raindrops. But Sableye crawled quickly around on the ceiling, dodging them all.

Then . . . *WHAM!* Sableye jumped down from the ceiling and slammed into Torchic. The little Pokémon swooned, then fell down in a faint.

May held out her Poké Ball. "Torchic, return now!"

Meowth stepped out of the shadows and slipped behind Sableye. "Nice job, Sableye. Slick scaring, kid!"

"Meowth?" Max said, surprised.

"What are you doing in this cave?" May asked.

Meowth grinned. "Not that it's any of your beeswax," it said. "But I'm here to push this button!"

Meowth opened its paw to reveal a small remote. It pressed a red button, and a net fell from the ceiling. Max and May were trapped.

"Get us out of here!" they yelled.

Team Rocket Rolls In

4

Ash and Pikachu caught up to Corphish. Then they met up with Brock outside the mine.

"Guess your plan failed," Brock said.

"Yeah, instead of acting brave, Corphish just got mad," Ash said.

"*Pika!*" Pikachu agreed.

Ash looked around. "Anyway, where are Max and May?"

"They haven't come out yet," Brock said.

"But they should have been out by now," Ash said, worried.

Brock nodded. "We'd better go inside and look."

Ash, Brock, and Pikachu walked back down the tunnel leading into the mine. Meowth and Sableye watched from the control room. Max and May were still trapped in the net, which hung from the ceiling.

"Let's go, kid," Meowth said to Sableye. "We've got some more scarin' to do!"

"*Sableye!*" Sableye agreed.

Ash had no idea they were being watched. Corphish wouldn't even look at Ash as they walked through the mine. The Water-type Pokémon was still angry about being tricked.

"How long are you going to stay mad, Corphish?" Ash asked. "It's partly your fault that Max and May got lost."

Corphish glared at Ash.

"I don't think you needed to point that out," Brock said.

The sound of rolling wheels floated down the tunnel. Ash looked up to see a mining cart slowly rolling toward them.

"I bet that's May and Max!" Ash cried. He ran toward the cart and looked in. "It's empty. Darn!"

While Ash looked in the cart, Sableye hung upside-down from the ceiling. It quickly licked the back of Ash's neck, then vanished back into the darkness.

"Was that you, Pikachu?" Ash asked, jumping up.

"*Pikachu,*" the Pokémon replied, shaking its head.

"Then if it wasn't you, who?" Ash wondered.

A low, rumbling sound filled the tunnel. Brock walked up to Ash.

"Did you hear that?" Brock asked.

Sableye swung down and licked Brock's neck. Then it quickly disappeared.

"Ah!" Brock cried out. "I just felt something touch my neck!"

"I felt that, too!" Ash said.

Meowth crept up behind Corphish. Then it quickly smacked Corphish's shell with its paw.

"*Corphish!*" The Water-type Pokémon spun around. It didn't see Meowth — but it saw Pikachu next to it. It thought Pikachu had hit it.

"*Corphish Corphish!*" Angry, Corphish tackled Pikachu.

"Pika!" Pikachu jumped to its feet and ran right at Corphish. Corphish pushed Pikachu back.

"Hey, Corphish, knock it off!" Brock yelled.

Ash frowned. Something weird was happening!

Max and May watched the whole scene from the control room. There was nothing they could do to help. Then May had an idea. She grabbed a Poké Ball from her belt.

"Torchic, go!"

Torchic popped out of the ball and landed on the floor. It wobbled on its feet.

"Looks like Torchic hasn't recovered from the last battle you guys had," Max said.

"Torchic, could you please use ember to burn this net?" May asked.

Torchic didn't let them down. It sprayed a small shower of Embers onto the net. The hot sparks burned through the ropes. The net opened up, and Max and May tumbled to the floor.

May held out her Poké Ball. "Thanks, Torchic. Now get some rest!"

The Fire-type Pokémon vanished inside the ball. Max turned to his sister.

"Let's go help Ash and Brock!" he said.

Down in the tunnel, Corphish and Pikachu were getting angrier and angrier.

Zap! Pikachu hurled a lightning bolt at Corphish. Corphish jumped.

Slam! Corphish attacked Pikachu with Bubblebeam. Pikachu jumped out of the way.

Meowth jumped out of the shadows. It aimed a small Blaster at Pikachu and Corphish. A net shot out of the blaster, trapping the two Pokémon.

"Meowth!" Ash yelled.

"We just caught them fair and square!" Meowth said with glee.

"Sableye! Sableye!" The spooky Pokémon stepped up next to Meowth.

"Look, it's a Sableye!" Brock cried. "I bet those two are the ones who were sneaking up on us back there."

"But what is a Sableye doing hanging out with Meowth?" Ash wondered.

Meowth laughed. "We're best friends! Friends till the end!"

Max and May arrived, speeding down the track in a mining cart.

"Sableye, don't believe anything Meowth says!" May yelled. "Meowth is only trying to trick you!"

"Yeah, he's just using you to capture Pikachu and other Pokémon," Max added.

Sableye turned to Meowth. *"Sableye?"* it asked.

"No, that's not true," Meowth protested. "I just wanted to hang out with you so we could have fun playing."

"Sableye?" Sableye didn't sound so sure.

"Don't trust Meowth, no matter what!" May said.

"I bet you didn't know that Meowth is a member of Team Rocket, did you?" Max asked.

Sableye held its head, confused.

"I'm not a liar," Meowth said desperately. "They're stinking, rotten liars and they're trying to trick you. So take care of them, pronto!"

Sableye didn't know what to do. Before it could make up its mind, a voice traveled down the tunnel.

"Prepare for trouble as we glide into view!"

"Make it double, 'cause that's what we do!"

Ash looked down the tunnel. Jessie, James, and Wobbuffet were riding a mining cart, coming from the opposite direction.

"Team Rocket!" Ash cried.

James grinned. "Sad to say, we found no treasure."

"But catching Pikachu is treasure enough!" Jessie cried.

Jessie reached out of the cart and grabbed the net from Meowth.

Meowth jumped into the cart. "The jig is up! Bye!"

Team Rocket put the mining cart in reverse. They zoomed toward the mine entrance.

"Time to say good-bye, twerps! Good-bye!" they called out.

Cave In!

Ash quickly pulled a Poké Ball from his belt.

"Taillow, let's go!" he yelled.

Taillow flew out of the ball and raced down the tunnel. It landed on top of Jessie's head and started pecking at her magenta hair.

"Stop, you're going to ruin my hair!" Jessie yelled. "It's a lot of work to get it this way!" She held up a black ball with a red letter *R* on it.

"But, Jessie, sweetheart . . ." James warned.

But Jessie didn't listen. She threw the ball at Taillow.

Bam! The ball exploded. Team Rocket went rolling off into the cave.

The walls of the cave began to shake. Rocks started to fall from the ceiling.

"Thanks for the warning, Jess," James grumbled. "Let's get out of here!"

Inside the cave, Taillow flew back to Ash. The friends huddled together as the mine caved in around them.

"There's no way out!" May cried.

Sableye tapped Ash on the shoulder. It pointed to a nearby tunnel.

"I think it wants to help," Ash said.

Outside the mine, Team Rocket brushed dirt and dust from their white uniforms.

"Well, that was close," Jessie said.

"If that little shock wave you sent hadn't blown us out of the mine, we would have bought the farm, too!" James said angrily.

Meowth ignored them. He stared at the mine entrance. Stones blocked the opening. Anyone inside would be trapped — forever.

"Wow, I feel bad, tricking Sableye like that," Meowth said sadly.

"Well, *I* don't feel bad," Jessie said.

"Right," James agreed. "It wasn't *our* fault."

"Of course, it was all your fault!" a voice yelled.

Team Rocket looked up. Ash and his friends stood on a ridge on top of the mine entrance. Sableye stood with them.

"The twerps!" Jessie cried.

"They're safe!" James said.

"And Sableye is okay, too!" Meowth added.

"Yeah, we're safe," Ash said. "But no thanks to you. Sableye showed us a way out."

"*Sableye!*" the Pokémon called down to Team Rocket.

"What's it saying?" James asked.

"It's saying that the ones who destroyed its favorite place to play are in big trouble!" said Meowth.

Sableye jumped down from the ridge. It used its hands to cut through the net holding Pikachu and Corphish. The two Pokémon ran out, free.

"Corphish, Crabhammer! Pikachu, Iron Tail!" Ash shouted.

Corphish's right claw glowed as it prepared for the attack. Pikachu somersaulted down from the ridge. Its tail glowed brightly.

Wham! Corphish hit Team Rocket with Crabhammer.

Bam! Pikachu smacked them with Iron Tail.

Sableye joined in. An eerie black light beamed from its eyes. The light rays slammed into Team Rocket with amazing force. Jessie, James, Meowth, and Wobbuffet went flying over the hills.

"Looks like Team Rocket's blasting off again!" they cried.

Ash, Brock, Max, and May climbed down from the ridge.

"Thank goodness that's over and everyone's safe," Ash said.

"Yeah, and we owe it all to Sableye," Brock pointed out.

Sableye climbed back up the ridge. It turned and faced the others. Corphish and Pikachu waved to Sableye. The Darkness Pokémon waved back.

"Even Corphish is thanking Sableye," Max remarked.

"Yeah," Ash said. "Maybe Corphish learned something today after all."

"*Corphish!*" the Water-type Pokémon agreed.

Ash waved up to Sableye.

"So long, Sableye," he called out. "I hope we see you again someday."

Sableye smiled. It could always find a new place to play. But today it had found something even better — true friends.

"*Sableye!*"

The Mysterious Mansion

6

After meeting Sableye, Ash and his friends contin-
ued on their journey. They met lots of new Pokémon
and battled Team Rocket again and again. Ash's Taillow
evolved into a Swellow. They did not encounter any
Pokémon as spooky as Sableye — until one stormy night.

It all started one day after Team Rocket tried to capture Pikachu — again. James set off a Bomber Beam that
sent Team Rocket blasting off.

Team Rocket flew through the sky . . . and crash
landed in front of a huge mansion. Tall trees and dark
woods surrounded the place.

Jessie groaned and stood up. "Not again!" she yelled. "We were just one inch away from catching Pikachu!"

"It's your fault, James," Meowth said. "Why did you go and flip the Bomber Beam up to full blast?"

"Because the plan was for you to get Pikachu into the hole. I had to do something, because you didn't do your job!" James snapped.

"Maybe 'cause this is how I nail my job!" Meowth cried. Then it swiped at James's face with its sharp claws.

"Oh, yeah? Well, I prefer knuckles!" James shot back. Then he smacked Meowth in the face.

Meowth jumped up to attack James and accidentally kicked Jessie in the face.

"Hey, nobody touches my face!" Jessie shrieked.

Jessie, James, and Meowth rolled around on the ground, fighting and yelling at each other. As they scuffled, a small Pokémon watched from behind a nearby bush.

Red beams of light glowed from the Pokémon's eyes. The light beams covered Team Rocket. They suddenly stopped fighting.

"I feel so refreshed and happy!" Meowth purred.

"Strange," Jessie said, smiling. "I hated you both moments ago."

"Yes, I hated you, too!" James said.

"Why were we fighting in the first place?" Meowth wondered. "We're pals."

Team Rocket stood together and cheered.

"Living large and standing tall.

"Who's the team that has it all?

"Team Rocket!"

James rubbed his belly. "Wow, a good friendship can sure work up an appetite."

Meowth pointed to the mansion. "A place like that has got to be filled with grub. And it doesn't look like anyone is home."

Jessie grinned. "Do your thing, Meowth!"

Meowth walked up to the big wooden door. It stuck its claws into the lock. Within seconds, the door swung open.

"Brilliant!" James cried.

"Aw, shucks," Meowth said. "Anyone could do that."

The three Pokémon thieves stepped inside the door. They found themselves in a huge hallway with a red carpet stretched in front of them.

"Nice place," Jessie remarked.

Suddenly, the big door slammed shut behind them. Jessie, James, and Meowth jumped.

"What happened?" James wondered. He ran to the door and tried to open it. It wouldn't budge.

"Meowth will save the day!" Jessie said.

"That's my cue," Meowth said. "Just a few Fury Swipes, and . . ."

Meowth attacked the door with all of its sharp claws. It scratched and scratched — but the door would not open.

"James, free us!" Jessie wailed.

"How? Magic?" James wondered.

"Jessie, it was your idea to come in here," Meowth said.

"No, it wasn't," Jessie snapped. "It was your idea!"

Team Rocket argued again. The small Pokémon that

had seen them outside watched them from the shadows. It hit them with red beams of light again.

Once again, Team Rocket stopped fighting.

"Let's not worry," Jessie said. "What do you say we
take a little look around this mansion."

"I'm in," James said.

"Off we go, then!" Meowth cried.

Team Rocket walked down the long hallway. From
its hiding place, the little Pokémon watched ... and
waited.

A Sudden Storm

7

While Team Rocket explored the mansion, Ash and his friends were trying to find the next town. Max led the group with his PokéNav, a handheld computer programmed with maps. But Max wasn't an expert at it yet.

The group came to a fork in the road. They could go left or right.

Max stopped. "There's no fork in the road on the PokéNav," he said.

"Well, since we're lost, anyway, let's try left!" Ash said.

"I guess it doesn't matter at this point," May said glumly.

Ash, Pikachu, and May took the left-hand turn.

"Hey, where are you going?" Max yelled. "I don't have any idea where that road leads to!"

"Neither do we," Brock pointed out. "Come on, let's go!"

The friends walked down the trail. Before long, dark clouds gathered in the sky above them. Thunder rumbled in the distance. Then cold rain poured down from the clouds.

"This stinks!" May complained. "This wouldn't have happened if we hadn't got lost."

Brock pointed down the trail. "Look! A nice warm house straight ahead!"

"Awesome!" Ash said. "Maybe we can go inside and dry out a bit."

They ran up to the door and knocked. Nobody answered.

"Maybe nobody lives here," Brock said. "It looks like a pretty old house."

"Yeah," May said, shivering. "And it's starting to give me the creeps, too."

Max chuckled. "Maybe this house is haunted!"

"That's not funny, Max," May said. "Stop it!"

Suddenly, the door swung open.

"Look," Max said. "They're inviting us inside."

"Are you sure?" May asked nervously.

Boom! Thunder crashed loudly. A jagged lightning bolt lit up the sky.

"Aaaah!" May shrieked, startled. She ran inside the house. The others followed her.

Bam! The door slammed shut behind them.

Ash ran to the door. "It's locked!"

Brock examined the door. He noticed the scratches left by Meowth's Fury Swipes. "Check that out," Brock remarked.

"Guys, I'm scared," May said. "I knew we never should have come into a creepy haunted house like this. Max, find us a way out of here!"

"What are you talking about?" Max snapped. "You're the one who came running in here in the first place."

"It's not my fault you have the PokéNav and you don't know how to use it," May shot back.

Ash stepped between them. "Come on, you guys," he said. "Stop it!"

"Pika! Pika!" Pikachu agreed.

"Look, maybe you can save your sibling rivalry for another time," Brock suggested.

May turned away from Max. "Fine!" she said. "The last thing I need is a know-it-all brother, anyway."

Max looked hurt. "You don't mean that, do you?"

"Yes, I do!" May said. "You think you know everything!"

"You're so mean!" Max yelled. "I hate you, May!"

Max ran down the hallway through a set of doors. They slammed shut behind him.

"Max, come back!" Ash yelled.

He and Brock ran to the doors. Just like the front door, they were locked.

"We need to find a way to get to Max," Brock said.

May was still smarting from their argument. "Let the brainiac take care of himself!"

"I don't think you really mean that," Brock said.

Max heard the whole conversation from behind the doors. May's words stung worse than a sting from a Beedrill.

"If she doesn't need me, then I don't need her," Max said. He turned and found himself in another hallway, lined with windows. He stomped down the hall. "Without me, she wouldn't even know how to tie her shoes! Sisters are so nasty sometimes! I just wish . . ."

Suddenly, Max felt his anger melt away.

"That's weird," Max said. "I know I was mad just a second ago. What happened?"

Then Max saw something out of the corner of his eye. A reflection in the window. As he focused on it, he realized it was a Pokémon, floating in the air. The Pokémon was gray, with a round head and big round eyes. Its head came to a point at the top. It didn't have arms or legs, just a loose body that flowed underneath its head like a sheet.

"Cool!" Max said. He turned to face the Pokémon. "You're a Shuppet, right?"

"*Shuppet! Shup, shup, Shuppet!*" the Pokémon answered in a happy voice.

"Hi, I'm Max," Max said. "It's nice to meet you."

Shuppet quickly disappeared. Max spun around. "Where'd you go?"

Shuppet appeared in front of Max's face and giggled.

"I think you're in the mood to play, aren't you?" Max asked.

Shuppet nodded. It floated down the hallway. Max followed it down a long staircase. Suddenly, he tripped.

"Whoa!" Max cried.

Shuppet turned to Max. A blue light surrounded Max's body. It lifted him in the air and deposited him gently at the bottom of the stairs.

"Thanks, Shuppet!" Max said. "How cool! You used Psychic on me."

"*Shuppet shup!*" the Pokémon replied.

Shuppet led Max through a door into a library. The walls were lined with tall bookshelves.

"Are you going to show me your favorite books?" Max wondered.

Shuppet didn't answer. Its eyes glowed with blue light. One of the bookcases opened up, like a door.

Shuppet led Max into a secret room, filled with toys and rides. Max saw a slide, swings, and even a small carousel.

"I can't believe it!" Max cried. "It's a carnival inside a house!"

Max climbed to the top of the slide. Shuppet sat in his lap. The two slid down, giggling.

"This is awesome!" Max said.

Then Max heard a familiar voice coming down the hallway.

"Maaax! Where are you?" May yelled. "You've made your point. Quit messing around and get out here already!"

"Hey, that's my sister," Max told Shuppet.

"Sorry, May," Ash said in the hallway. "You must be getting worried about Max, right?"

"Why? I'm not worried at all," May said. "He'll come crying to me once he gets hungry!"

"She doesn't care," Max told Shuppet. "If that's the way she wants it, fine!"

Max turned to his new friend. "Shuppet, I have an idea. . . ."

Scaring with Shuppet

8

Ash, Pikachu, Brock, and May looked throughout the house for Max, but they couldn't find him.

"Say something Max!" Brock yelled.

The friends walked into a dining room. There was a round table in the corner, covered with a tablecloth and dishes. A tall hutch against the wall held fancy cups and plates.

"I don't see Max," May said.

Bam! The dining room door shut behind them.

"Ha!" May said nervously. "Must have been the wind."

"That's right," Ash said. He was feeling nervous, too.

"Anyway, we'll just say it was," Brock suggested.

Then the curtains on the windows started to flap.

"Is it the wind again?" May asked.

Brock examined the windows. "Maybe, but the window is closed!"

Under the round table, hidden by the tablecloth, Max giggled. His plan was working! He and Shuppet were giving May a real scare.

"Ready, Shuppet? Next trick," Max said.

"Shuppet shup!" the little Pokémon whispered. It used Psychic to make the hutch full of dishes rattle and shake.

"I know the window is closed," May said. "But there must be a crack somewhere, right?"

"Good thinking," Brock said.

The plates and cups flew off of the hutch. They twirled and danced in midair.

"Pikachu!" Pikachu yelled.

"That is *definitely* not the wind!" Ash agreed.

"Let's get out of here!" May screamed.

Shuppet used Psychic to swing the door open, and

Ash, Pikachu, Brock, and May ran out as fast as they could. Max rolled on the floor, laughing.

"They're scared out of their wits!" he cried.

May led the others down the hallway in a panic.

"I've got to get out of this house — whoa!"

May bumped into a woman with short brown hair. They collided in the hall and fell to the floor. The woman jumped to her feet, angry.

"Who are you?" she demanded. "Why did you break into my house and scratch up the front door?"

"That's not how it happened!" May protested.

Brock stepped forward and held out his hand. "Hi there. My name is Brock. It's true we did let ourselves in, but only to get out of the rain. The door was already scratched when we entered."

The woman looked suspicious.

Brock's dark eyes started to shine, just like they did whenever he saw a pretty woman. "But it's obvious to me now that it was fate that ordained you and me to meet in this very house. . . ."

May grabbed Brock by the ear and dragged him

away. "Just like it's fate for me to take over for Max!" she said. Max was usually the one who kept Brock in line when he got goofy over girls.

"My name is Emily," the woman said. "Why don't you tell me what's going on?"

"Sure," Ash said. He told Emily everything that had happened since they came into the house.

"So strange things have been happening again," Emily said. She didn't seem surprised. "And now your brother's missing?"

"What do you mean, strange things are happening again?" May asked.

"I have been wanting to remodel this house for the longest time," Emily explained. "But all of these strange things keep on happening. Doors slam shut, things fly around. . . ."

"It's definitely happening again!" Ash said.

Emily frowned. "Every time I try to hire someone to do work on this place, they always turn me down. I'll never turn the mansion into a hotel."

"You want to make a hotel out of a haunted house?" May asked.

"May, cool it," Brock warned.

Emily smiled weakly. "It's fine. I've heard that before. It's just sad. I used to live here when I was a little girl. The house was so beautiful then. I'd like to make it beautiful again."

"Sounds like a good idea," Brock said.

Emily frowned. "But if these strange things keep happening . . ."

May suddenly felt afraid for her brother. "We've got to find Max, now!" she cried.

Ash nodded. "Especially now that we know creepy stuff is going on."

"Let's split up and have another look," Brock suggested.

May threw out a Poké Ball. "Torchic! I choose you!" she yelled. The little Fire-type Pokémon popped out.

"Swellow, you come out, too!" Ash yelled. His Flying-type Pokémon flew out of its Poké Ball.

"Let's go, Mudkip!" Brock cried. The cute Water-type Pokémon burst out of its Poké Ball.

Ash looked at the Pokémon. "You have to help us find Max," he said.

The Pokémon nodded. Then they took off in different directions.

May looked after them, worried. "I hope Max is okay!"

Team Rocket Attacks!

9

Max climbed out from under the table. "I had so much fun playing with you, Shuppet," Max said.

"*Shuppet Shuppet!*" the Pokémon agreed.

Then he heard voices. He quickly ducked back under the table, leaving just enough room to peek out from under the tablecloth.

Team Rocket walked into the room, arguing about how lost they were.

"If it wasn't for Jessie, we wouldn't have set foot inside this dump!" said James, rubbing his stomach.

Jessie snapped back, "Correction, your empty stomach led us here and then Meowth let us in!"

Meowth jumped up. "Keep Meowth out of this!"

On the other side of the room, Torchic stepped through the front door.

"*Torchic? Torchic tor?*"

"That's May's Torchic," Max whispered. "If she's using her Torchic to find me, maybe she does care after all."

"Look," Jessie said, pointing. "It's that twerp's Torchic!"

"But now it's Team Rocket's Torchic!" Meowth said gleefully.

Torchic turned around, surprised to find itself face-to-face with Team Rocket. They advanced toward the little Fire-type Pokémon.

"What do I do?" Max whispered. "If I don't do something, Torchic will get caught."

He almost didn't care. May did love Torchic. But she said such mean things to him! He wasn't ready to forgive her.

James sneered at Torchic. "You can make this easy or difficult," he warned.

Torchic backed up, step by step. Soon the Fire Pokémon backed into a wall. It was trapped!

I don't care, Max told himself. *What has May ever done for me, anyway?*

As soon as he had the thought, memories flooded into Max's mind, like May taking care of Max when he was sick.

All of his angry feelings melted away. May was his sister. He wasn't going to let Team Rocket hurt her!

Max ran out from under the table.

"You guys better leave Torchic alone!" Max cried.

"Torchic!" the little Pokémon agreed.

Shuppet flew out and floated next to Max. Together, they faced Team Rocket.

But the villains just smiled.

"Ah, it's the littlest twerp of all," Meowth said.

"But who's the pointy Pokémon?" Jessie wondered.

James took some index cards from his pocket and flipped through them. "Aha! It's a Shuppet, the Puppet Pokémon," he read out loud. "It supposedly grows by absorbing human anger, and various other attitudes."

"Shuppet! It was you who stopped me from feeling upset back there," Max realized.

"That must have been what happened to us," James said.

"Let's catch Shuppet, too," Jessie said. "We'll give it to the Boss. He's the angriest person I know!"

"We'll make it a two-for-one catch," Meowth said.

Max quickly grabbed Torchic. "My sister loves this Torchic more than anything," he said. "No way am I going to let you creeps get ahold of it."

Jessie sneered. "That's touching — but dumb."

"You can't fight the three of us," James said.

May ran in the door and stood next to Max. "Like he would listen to you!" she said.

Max beamed. "May, you came!"

"My brother never listens to anybody, he's so busy yakking all the time," May said. "But still, he's the only brother I've got, and I love him."

Max smiled. "I love you, too, May."

"How nice," Jessie sneered. "I may throw up."

Then Jessie threw a Poké Ball into the air.

"Seviper, let's go!" she yelled.

A Psychic Save

10

A fierce-looking Pokémon flew out of Jessie's Poké Ball. Seviper, a Poison-type Pokémon, looked like a long black snake with sharp fangs.

"Cacnea, you, too!" James yelled. He threw a Poké Ball, and a round green Pokémon with sharp spikes all over its body came out. Cacnea immediately hugged James's face.

"Ouch! Cacnea, stop!" James shrieked.

"Now, Seviper, use Bite attack!" Jessie commanded.

Seviper launched itself toward Max and May, its sharp fangs bared.

"Quick attack, Torchic!" May yelled.

Torchic jumped up and slammed into Seviper's chest. The little Pokémon's attack packed a lot of power. It knocked Seviper onto the floor.

"Cacnea, Pin Missile!" James cried.

Cacnea jumped off of James and faced Torchic. It shot sharp, needlelike spikes at the Fire-type Pokémon.

"Now use ember!" May told Torchic.

A barrage of white-hot Embers shot out of Torchic's beak. They knocked the pins right out of the air.

"Poison Tail, Seviper!" Jessie yelled.

Seviper lashed at Torchic with its thick, powerful tail.

"Dodge, Torchic!" May cried.

Torchic dodged out of the way. Seviper's tail slammed into the heavy hutch. The hutch toppled over — and Max was right underneath! May ran and grabbed Max, trying to protect him.

"Max, get down!" May yelled as she shielded her brother.

But Shuppet acted quickly. It used Psychic on the

hutch. The heavy piece of furniture glowed with blue light. It stopped moving just in time. Then it rested back against the wall. May and Max were safe!

May smiled at Shuppet. "That was awesome! Thanks!"

"Shup Shuppet shup!"

Swellow flew into the room. Ash, Pikachu, Brock, Mudkip, and Emily ran in behind it.

"Are you okay?" Brock asked.

"We're fine, thanks to our friend Shuppet," Max said proudly.

Emily's eyes got wide when she saw Shuppet. "Could it be . . ." she wondered.

Team Rocket was annoyed by the interruption.

"Couldn't you twerps break into someone else's house?" Jessie asked.

"We were here first!" James said.

"Which means everything in this house is ours," Meowth added.

Shuppet gave Team Rocket an angry look. The dishes on the table suddenly glowed with blue light and flew at

Team Rocket like missiles. They screamed and ducked.

"I get it now," Brock said. "Shuppet was using Psychic the whole time. That's why all these strange things have been happening."

Emily stepped forward. "I remember," she said. "Shuppet and I used to play here together when I was a little girl."

Emily looked into Shuppet's eyes. "See, Shuppet? It's Emily! But I'm all grown up now!"

Shuppet nodded. *"Shuppet shup!"*

"I've missed you, too," Emily said. She gave Shuppet a hug.

Team Rocket got teary-eyed.

"Such a beautiful reunion," Jessie said. "But the mush has gone on long enough! Let's see how a little netting grabs you!"

In a flash, Jessie grabbed Shuppet in a net. Then she jumped out the window, followed by James and Meowth. The villains landed in their Meowth-shaped balloon, which hovered right outside the window.

"Prepare for trouble as we float away," Jessie said.

"Make it double, as I like to say!" James added.

Jessie and James launched into the Team Rocket motto.

To protect the world from devastation,
To unite all peoples within our nation,
To denounce the evils of truth and love,
To extend our reach to the stars above!
Jessie! James!
Team Rocket blasts off at the speed of light!
Surrender now along with your Shuppet,
Or prepare for a fight, fight, fight!"

Meowth grinned. "Meowth, that's right!"

"Wobbuffet!" the blue Pokémon added, appearing behind Jessie.

"Swellow, go and bring Shuppet back!" Ash yelled.

Swellow flew out the window, aimed at the balloon.

"Cacnea, use Pin Missile!" James commanded.

Cacnea shot the sharp missiles at Swellow.

"Dodge and use Wing Attack!" Ash cried.

Swellow dodged the Pin Missile. Its wings glowed

as they gathered power for the attack. It swiped its wings at the net holding Shuppet. The net broke, and Shuppet floated free. Swellow flew away from the balloon.

"Now, Pikachu, use Thunder attack, go!" Ash yelled.

Pikachu jumped up. It rocked the balloon with a powerful shock.

"Team Rocket's blasting off again!" they cried. The balloon disappeared over the horizon.

Max and May faced each other.

"I'm sorry, May," Max said. "I know I said some things that weren't very nice."

"I'm the one who should be sorry," May said. "I'm your big sister. I should never have been so mean to you."

"You're also the greatest sister a guy could ever have," Max said.

"Really?" May asked.

Max grinned. "Of course, you are still a girl!"

"Oh, yeah? What's wrong with that?" May teased.

Brock smiled. "Looks like they finally patched things up."

"That's a relief," Max agreed.

Emily turned to the friends. "Shuppet and I are going to work together and turn this place into a wonderful hotel," she said. "I hope you'll come stay with us when it's ready."

"Sure!" everyone replied.

Max spoke to Shuppet. "Thanks for your help, Shuppet. I'm happy for you."

"Shuppet shup!"

The friends left Emily's mansion. May turned and looked back at the house.

"This place doesn't look so scary anymore," she said. "You know what was really scary?"

"What?" Max asked.

"Almost losing you," May said.

Max smiled. "Maybe Jessie was right. This is getting really mushy!"

"Pikachu!" Pikachu laughed.